THE EVERYDAY ADVENTURES OF Savvy & Rey

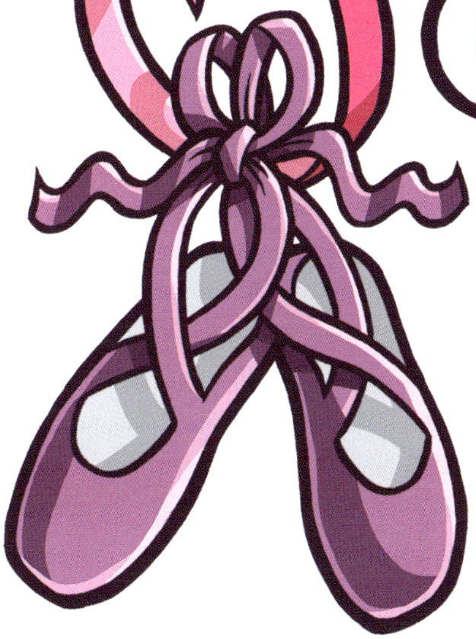

My First Day at Ballet

by Cristina O'Connell

illustrated by Kevin Cannon

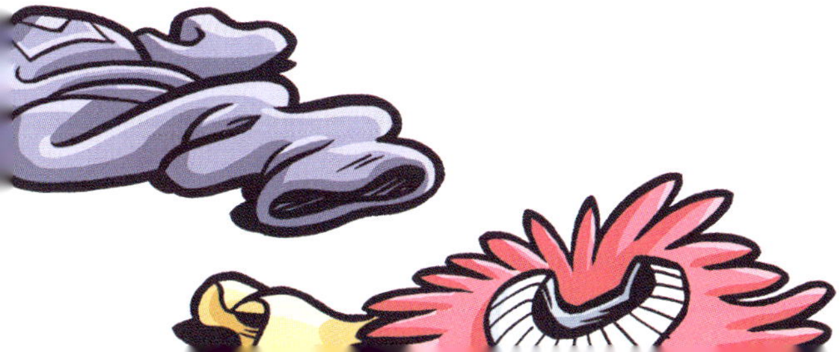

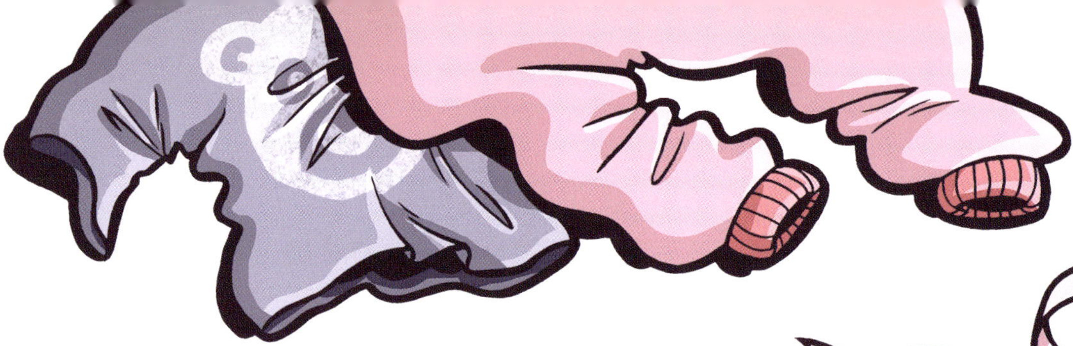

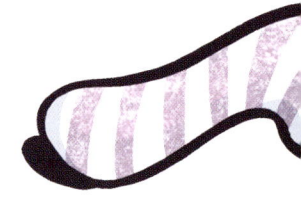

The Everyday Adventures of Savvy & Ry: My First Day at Ballet © copyright 2019 by Cristina O'Connell. All rights reserved. No part of this book may be reproduced in any form whatsoever, by photography or xerography or by any other means, by broadcast or transmission, by translation into any kind of language, nor by recording electronically or otherwise, without permission in writing from the author, except by a reviewer, who may quote brief passages in critical articles or reviews.

ISBN 13: 978-1-63489-223-0

Library of Congress Catalog Number: 2019936926

Printed in the United States of America
First Printing: 2019

23 22 21 20 19   5 4 3 2 1

Cover and interior illustration and design by Kevin Cannon

Wise Ink Creative Publishing
807 Broadway St. NE. #46
Minneapolis, MN 55413
wiseink.com

To order, visit www.adventuresofsavvyandry.com or contact Itasca Books at 1-800-901-3480 (itascabooks.com). Reseller discounts available.

This book is dedicated to all On Pointe dancers, past and present.
You have inspired me in so many ways. I hope you reach for
the stars and work hard to achieve your goals.

It was the first day of ballet class, and Savvy was ready with everything she needed: her bright pink leotard, sparkly tutu, and pink ballet slippers. The colors made her feel like a unicorn!

Savvy's full name was Savannah, but everyone called her Savvy.

"Savvy, make sure you buckle your seatbelt!" said Ry, Savvy's older brother, as they got into the car. Ry had been dancing for two years already. "Are you excited for your first lesson?"

"I sure am!" said Savvy.

When they got to the new ballet studio downtown, Savvy's excitement felt different. She had a tickle in her tummy, and she began wondering about the other kids in ballet class.

Would they like her? What if Savvy wasn't any good at ballet? Was the teacher nice?

They were greeted by a very kind lady.

"You must be Savvy! I'm Ms. Belle, and it's a pleasure to meet you. Are you ready to join me in your first ballet class?"

Savvy nodded, but did not say anything.

"Savvy, I almost forgot!" Mom said. "Ry and I picked out something very special for you to wear on your first day of dance." She pulled out a small box wrapped in sparkly wrapping paper.

"What is it?" Savvy asked.

"You'll just have to see!" said Ry. Ry was a very thoughtful big brother.

Savvy shook the box and felt something small bouncing around.

When she opened it, she found a bracelet
with a shiny silver ballet slipper on it.

"This is a very special ballet charm to wear to
dance class each week," Mommy said. "It's to
remind you to be brave, and to have FUN!"

"Thank you, Mommy! Thank you, Ry!" Savvy said. She could feel her tummy begin to settle.

"Ry and I will be watching you from right here!" said Mommy.

As Ry closed the door, Savvy felt the tickle in her tummy come back—and this time it went all the way to her toes! Savvy finally knew what she'd been feeling—she was nervous! "Wait, Mommy, don't leave me! I don't know anyone in class!"

Ms. Belle, who was very kind, leaned down to Savvy. "Oh Savvy, you are going to have so much fun twirling and leaping in class today. Everyone is a stranger until they become a friend!"

"But I'm scared!" Savvy said.

"This is where all of the little ballerinas like you come to learn! The mommies and daddies watch through the window," Ms. Belle said. "Look, Ry is already watching and waving to you!"

"Okay... I'm ready!" Savvy said.

She followed Ms. Belle into the dance room with the other kids.

First, Ms. Belle had the kids make a circle to introduce themselves. Savvy felt less nervous as she looked around at the other kids, who all seemed nervous, too. Savvy made a point to smile at each one. Then it was Savvy's turn . . . she rubbed her ballet slipper charm for good luck.

"Hello everyone! I'm Savvy, short for Savannah. I love rainbows, unicorns, and purple!"

Then it was time to stretch.

They stretched their toes . . .

Reached up to the sky . . .

Then reached back down.

Savvy thought stretching wasn't easy, but Ms. Belle said it was important.

"Now it's time to pretend that we are butterflies flying in the sky!" Ms. Belle said.

Everyone got to pick which color butterfly they wanted to be. Of course, Savvy chose to be a rainbow-colored butterfly.

Then it was time for a clapping game. "One, two, three, four, five, six, seven, eight!" They did it over and over... this was Savvy's favorite game so far.

Finally, it was time to dance!

Savvy went first and did a tendu across the floor.
"Nice pointed feet, Savvy!" Ms. Belle said.

Savvy forgot all about being nervous and started having so much fun dancing!

The kids galloped across the room until class was almost over, but Ms. Belle had one more surprise.

"Time for freeze dance!" Ms. Belle said.

After ballet class, Savvy joined her new friends, Mia and Kayla, in line for stickers from Ms. Belle.

"You did a super job!" said Ms. Belle as she handed Savvy a sticker and gave her a hug. "Make sure you practice your tendu, and I'll see you next week!"

Savvy smiled as she skipped out the door.

"Savvy, you did a great job." Ry said.

"Thanks, Ry—my new ballet charm gave me the courage and strength I needed to believe in myself!" Savvy said.

"I think you had the courage and strength to do your best all along—you just needed to find it right in here," Mommy said, as she put her hand on Savvy's heart.

"I wonder what our next dancing adventure will be?" Mommy said.